SPOTLIGHT ON SOCIAL AND EMOTIONAL LEARNING

# ACKNOWLEDGING YOUR THOUGHTS AND FEELINGS

## REFLECTING



RACHAEL MORLOCK

PowerKiDS press™

NEW YORK

Published in 2020 by The Rosen Publishing Group, Inc.
29 East 21st Street, New York, NY 10010



Editor: Rachel Gintner
Designer: Michael Flynn

Photo Credits: Cover Tetra Images/Brand X Pictures/Getty Images; cover, pp. 1, 3–4, 6–12, 14–16, 18–20, 22–24 (background) TairA/Shutterstock.com; p. 4 markara/Shutterstock.com; p. 5 Soloviova Liudmyla/Shutterstock.com; p. 6 Pukhov K/Shutterstock.com; p. 7 marekuliasz/Shutterstock.com; p. 9 Prostock-studio/Shutterstock.com; p. 10 Maryna Patzen/Shutterstock.com; pp. 11, 19 Monkey Business Images/Shutterstock.com; pp. 13, 15 Bettmann/Getty Images; p. 14 Ariane Hoehne/Shutterstock.com; p. 16 Everett Historical/Shutterstock.com; p. 17 Shaun Tandon/AFP/Getty Images; p. 18 Busyok Creative/Shutterstock.com; p. 21 Philipp Kester/ullstein bild Dtl/Getty Images; p. 22 Ilike/Shutterstock.com.

Cataloging-in-Publication Data

Names: Morlock, Rachael.
Title: Acknowledging your thoughts and feelings: reflecting / Rachael Morlock.
Description: New York : PowerKids Press, 2020. | Series: Spotlight on social and emotional learning | Includes glossary and index.
Identifiers: ISBN 9781725306448 (pbk.) | ISBN 9781725306479 (library bound) | ISBN 9781725306455 (6pack)
Subjects: LCSH: Self-actualization (Psychology)--Juvenile literature.
Identity (Psychology)--Juvenile literature.
Classification: LCC BF637.S4 M675 2020 | DDC 158.1--dc23

Manufactured in the United States of America

CPSIA Compliance Information: Batch #CWPK20. For further information contact Rosen Publishing, New York, New York at 1-800-237-9932.

# CONTENTS

CHAPTER ONE

# THE EXAMINED LIFE

A **philosopher** named Socrates in ancient Greece is said to have claimed, "The unexamined life is not worth living." Socrates believed that his purpose as a human being was to question and **examine** life. This practice of thinking carefully and seriously is also known as reflection.

Reflection is an important tool for building stronger connections. You can use reflection to learn more about the people around you and yourself. When you take time to reflect on your thoughts and feelings, you're more likely to understand why you have them and what to do about them.

Reflection is also a tool for making better decisions. It offers a way to look back on your past in order to improve the future. Reflection helps you learn from your mistakes. Everything you need for reflection is already within you. It just takes practice!

SOCRATES

Usually, taking some quiet time to think is the best way to reflect on your thoughts, feelings, and decisions.

# CHAPTER TWO

# SELF-AWARENESS

Reflecting is part of self-awareness, or how you see yourself. Self-awareness helps you understand who you are, what you need, and what your goals are. It gives you a clear idea of your strengths and weaknesses. It helps you understand how you're feeling and why. Self-awareness also gives you a clearer idea of how others see you. When you're self-aware, it's easier to take charge of your feelings and make healthy choices.

Self-reflection is about taking a good look at yourself. A mirror shows you how you look on the outside, but self-reflection helps you understand what's happening on the inside.

Greater self-awareness comes from reflecting on your thoughts, feelings, and experiences. Have you ever felt a strong emotion without really knowing why? This is a good opportunity to reflect and understand yourself better. Think about what happened and how you felt. Ask yourself why you felt that way. Taking time to think carefully about your emotions is a way of reflecting on your life.

# CHAPTER THREE

# THOUGHTS AND FEELINGS

Your thoughts and feelings are part of who you are. Both positive and **negative** thoughts and feelings are a normal part of life. They might be **reactions** to changes in your life, your goals for the future, or your interactions with other people. Thoughts and feelings can be very powerful and sometimes **overwhelming**. In these times, it's especially helpful to sort through these feelings.

When you slow down to reflect, you can begin to understand more about yourself. Your thoughts and emotions give you clues about what's important to you, who you are, and who you want to be. The first step in reflecting is to acknowledge, or notice, your thoughts and feelings. Then, you can try to identify them. Can you name the emotions you're feeling? Much of the time, several emotions may be clustered together and may need to be untangled.

Identifying emotions is an important skill for gaining self-awareness. Can you recognize different emotions by the way they make you feel and by how you act?

# CHAPTER FOUR

# REFLECTION METHODS

Whether you're focusing on your thoughts, feelings, experiences, or decisions, there are different ways to reflect. An important key to reflection is creating a space where you're able to think. Some people might prefer to do this quietly on their own. Others might prefer to reflect by talking with a friend, teacher, or relative.

Your family could make a habit of reflecting together. At the dinner table, each of you can take a minute to think back on your day, and then you can take turns sharing the best and worst parts.

Sometimes, reflection just takes time to think. But if you're having trouble or you're not sure how to reflect, you can use tools to help. You can keep a journal to record your experiences and share your thoughts. You could also create a piece of art to show your feelings. Playing a special game might help you open up to sharing your thoughts and feelings with others. Once you find a method that works well for you, you can begin to make reflection a daily habit.

# CHAPTER FIVE

# REFLECTIVE DECISION-MAKING

In addition to helping you understand your thoughts and feelings, reflection also plays a role, or part, in making good decisions. Good decision-making follows a set of steps. First, you think of the situation and identify the dilemma, or problem. Next, you consider your options. After **evaluating** your options, you choose the best one. You've made your decision at this point, but the process isn't finished. The final step is to reflect on your choice.

Reflection requires you to look back and study the consequences, or results, of your decision. Reflection can help you make better choices next time. It can show you whether your actions were in line with your goals. The scientist Charles Darwin believed that people had a duty to reflect. He wrote, "A moral being is one who is capable of reflecting on his past actions and their **motives**—of approving of some and disapproving of others."

Darwin **developed** the idea of evolution by natural selection. This means that living things change over time based on features that help some survive. He also believed that people could change and improve by reflecting on their lives and choices.

CHAPTER SIX

# SELF-REFLECTION

It might take some time to see the consequences of your decisions, but it's never too late to reflect. Reflecting can help you find links between your actions and their results. You can reflect by thinking over what happened, what worked, and what didn't work. This prepares you for similar situations in the future.

The science fiction writer Ursula K. LeGuin wrote, "The only questions that really matter are the ones you ask yourself." Reflecting is asking yourself questions and thinking through the answers.

One good way to reflect is to ask yourself questions and try to find answers. What choice did you make? How did you make it? What were the positive results of your choice? What were the negative results? What worked and why? What didn't work and why? What do you know now that you didn't know then? What would you do differently next time? What thoughts and emotions were part of your choice? These questions can guide you to think carefully about a decision and its effects.

# CHAPTER SEVEN

# THE POWER OF MISTAKES

Reflecting involves learning as much as possible from experiences. You can learn from good experiences, but you can also learn from mistakes. In fact, mistakes are especially good at showing you ways you can improve. Reflection is a tool for **analyzing** and finding your mistakes.

You can make a mistake on your own or as part of a group. As an individual, it's important to name your misstep and say you're sorry. If you wrong a friend, you explain what happened and apologize. Large groups such as governments also have to do this when they make poor choices. For example, in 2011 the U.S. government acknowledged it was wrong to pass the Chinese Exclusion Act of 1882. This act hurt many Chinese **immigrants** and would-be immigrants to the United States. Reflecting on this act as a country could help us avoid similar mistakes in the future.

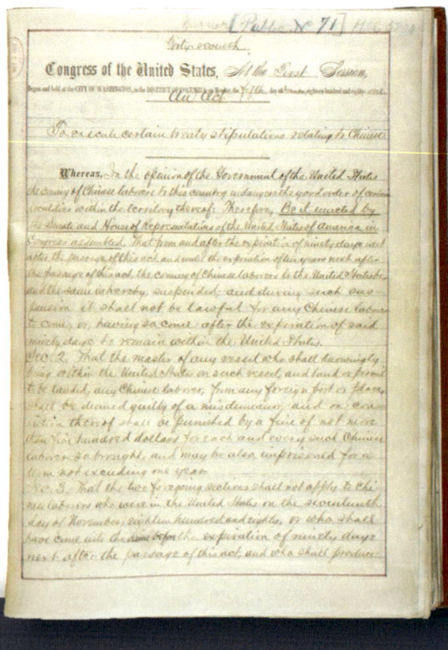
Congress of the United States,

CHINESE EXCLUSION ACT OF 1882

In this photograph from 2011, U.S. Representative Mike Coffman stands in front of a reproduced sign from 1892. Coffman and other U.S. officials publicly apologized to Chinese Americans for unfair practices of the past.

# CHAPTER EIGHT

# GROWTH MINDSET

The idea that mistakes help you learn is part of a growth mindset. Someone with a growth mindset believes that their abilities and skills improve over time through hard work. This is the opposite of someone with a fixed mindset. They believe that their intelligence and abilities stay the same no matter how hard they work. Science supports the idea of the growth mindset. It shows that human brains can change and develop through **dedication** and effort.

## FIXED MINDSET VS. GROWTH MINDSET

Someone with a fixed mindset feels limited by their mistakes. With a growth mindset, you can keep changing, growing, and developing new skills in spite of setbacks.

Having a growth mindset can motivate, or encourage, you to reflect on your life experiences, thoughts, emotions, and decisions. It shows you that mistakes and failures are not the end of the road. Instead, they offer helpful information about your strengths and weaknesses and how to reach your goals. Reflecting also shows how your thoughts and feelings change over time as you learn and grow.

# CHAPTER NINE

# REFLECTION IN ACTION

Self-awareness and social skills rely on reflection. Reflection helps you understand yourself, your choices, and your goals. It gives you time to look closely at your thoughts and feelings. Many religions teach reflection as a way for people to become more balanced and understanding.

Reflection is also part of learning. Scientists, mathematicians, artists, and students in all fields use reflection to grow. In science, reflection is an important step in experiments. It helps scientists draw connections between causes and effects.

Inventors practice reflection when they analyze mistakes and imagine new solutions. The Wright brothers tested seven different flying machines before they built a successful airplane. Reflection helped them come up with new plans and fine-tune old models until they found one that worked. What would have happened if the Wright brothers had given up instead of reflecting on their trials?

Crash after crash helped Wilbur and Orville Wright think about the weaknesses in their flying machines. They reflected on each attempt in order to improve.

CHAPTER TEN

# EVERYDAY REFLECTIONS

Reflection means thinking about how you feel, think, act, and learn. It's about looking back and analyzing what you see. Reflection can help you acknowledge your thoughts and feelings. It connects the lessons of the past with the choices of the future. It can help you reach your goals by giving you a clear idea of where you are, where you want to be, and what you can do to get there.

How can you make reflection part of your daily life? You might set aside time each day for reflection after school, at dinner, or before you go to bed. Have reflective talks with your friends and family and share your thoughts and feelings. Notice how the people you admire reflect on their lives. You have the power to learn and grow by tuning in to your own thoughts, feelings, and experiences.

# GLOSSARY

**analyze (AA-nuh-liyz)** To study something closely and carefully.

**dedication (deh-dih-KAY-shuhn)** The act of working hard for a cause.

**develop (dih-VEHL-uhp)** To bring out the possibilities of, to begin to have gradually, or to create over time.

**evaluate (ih-VAL-yuh-wayt)** To judge the importance, worth, or quality.

**examine (ig-ZAA-muhn)** To inspect or study carefully.

**immigrant (IH-muh-gruhnt)** A person who comes to a country to live there.

**motive (MOH-tiv)** A cause or reason to act.

**negative (NEH-guh-tiv)** Harmful or bad, also unwanted.

**overwhelming (oh-vuhr-WEHL-ming)** Something that is overpowering in thought and feeling.

**philosopher (fuh-LAH-suh-fuhr)** A person who studies philosophy, or the study of the basic ideas about knowledge, right and wrong, reasoning, and the value of things.

**reaction (ree-ACK-shuhn)** A response to something that happens, such as a change.

# INDEX



# PRIMARY SOURCE LIST

**Page 13**
Charles Darwin. Photograph. J. Cameron. 1869. Bettmann via Getty Images.

**Page 15**
Ursula K. LeGuin holding a book. Photograph. M. Klimek. December 20, 1985. Bettmann via Getty Images.

**Page 21**
Orville and Wilbur Wright. Photograph. Philipp Kester. January 1, 1909. Ullstein Bild via Getty Images.

# WEBSITES

Due to the changing nature of Internet links, PowerKids Press has developed an online list of websites related to the subject of this book. This site is updated regularly. Please use this link to access the list: www.powerkidslinks.com/SSEL/reflecting